LITTLE MISS
NAUGHTY

by Roger Hargreaves

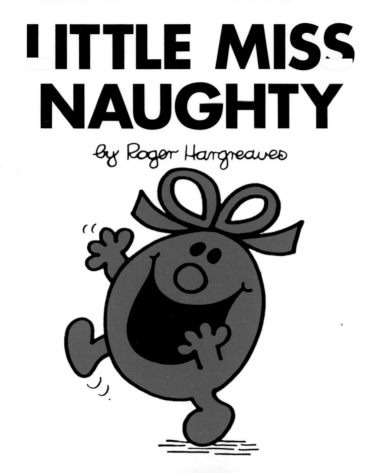

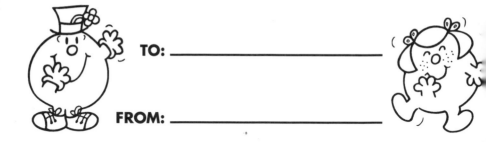

TO: _____

FROM: _____

LITTLE MISS NAUGHTY

by Roger Hargreaves

Grosset & Dunlap
An Imprint of Penguin Random House

Are you ever naughty?

Sometimes, I bet!

Well, Little Miss Naughty was naughty all the time.

She woke up one Sunday morning and looked out of the window.

"Looks like a nice day," she said to herself.

And then she grinned.

"Looks like a nice day for being naughty," she said.

And rubbed her hands!

That Sunday, Mr. Uppity was out for his morning stroll.

Little Miss Naughty knocked his hat off his head.

And jumped on it!

"My hat!" cried Mr. Uppity.

That afternoon, Mr. Clever was sitting in his garden reading a book.

And do you know what that Little Miss Naughty did?

She broke his glasses!

"My glasses!" cried Mr. Clever.

That evening, Mr. Bump was just standing there.

Minding his own business.

And guess what Little Miss Naughty did?

She ran off with his bandages!

And bandaged up Mr. Small!

"Mmmmmmmmmmmffffff!" he cried.

It's difficult to say anything when you're bandaged up like that!

Mr. Uppity and Mr. Clever and Mr. Bump and Mr. Small were very very very very cross.

Very very very very cross indeed!

"Oh what a wonderful Sunday," giggled Little Miss Naughty as she walked along. "And it isn't even bedtime yet!"

First thing on Monday morning, the Mr. Men had a meeting.

"Something has to be done," announced Mr. Uppity, who had managed to straighten out his hat.

They all looked at Mr. Clever, who was wearing his spare pair of glasses.

"You're the cleverest," they said. "What's to be done about Little Miss Naughty?"

Mr. Clever thought.

He cleared his throat.

And spoke.

"I have no idea," he said.

"I have," piped up Mr. Small.

"I know what that naughty little lady needs," he went on. "And I know who can do it," he added.

"What?" asked Mr. Uppity.

"Who?" asked Mr. Clever.

"Aha!" chuckled Mr. Small, and went off to see a friend of his.

Somebody who could do impossible things.

Somebody who could do impossible things like making himself invisible.

I wonder who that could be?

That Monday, Mr. Nosey was asleep under a tree.

Little Miss Naughty crept toward him with a pot of paint in one hand, a paintbrush in the other, and a rather large grin on her face.

She was going to paint the end of his nose!

Red!

But.

Just as she was about to do the dreadful deed, something happened.

TWEAK!

Somebody tweaked her nose!

Somebody she couldn't see tweaked her nose!

Somebody invisible!

I wonder who!

"Ouch!" cried Little Miss Naughty.

And, dropping the paint and paintbrush, she ran away as fast as her little legs would carry her.

One Tuesday, Mr. Busy was rushing along.

As usual!

Little Miss Naughty, standing by the side of the road, stuck out her foot.

She was going to trip him!

Head over heels!

And heels over head!

But.

Just before she did, something happened.

TWEAK!

The invisible nose tweaker had struck again!

And it hurt!

"Ouch!" cried Little Miss Naughty.

And ran away even faster than her little legs would carry her.

On Wednesday, Mr. Happy was at home.

Watching television!

Outside, Little Miss Naughty picked up a stone.

She was going to break his window!

Naughty girl!

But.

As she brought her arm back to throw, guess what?

That's right!

TWEAK!

"Ouch!" cried Little Miss Naughty as she ran off holding her nose.

And so it went on.

All day Thursday.

TWEAK!

All day Friday.

TWEAK! TWEAK!

All day Saturday.

TWEAK! TWEAK! TWEAK!

By which time Little Miss Naughty's nose was bright red.

But.

By Sunday she was cured.

No naughtiness at all!

Thanks to the invisible nose tweaker.

On Sunday evening, Mr. Small went to see him.

"Hello Mr. Impossible," he smiled. "Thank you for helping to cure Little Miss Naughty."

"My pleasure," laughed Mr. Impossible. "But it did take all week."

Mr. Small grinned.

"Don't you mean," he said, "all tweak?"

MR. MEN **LITTLE MISS**
by Roger Hargreaves

MR. MEN™ LITTLE MISS™
Copyright © THOIP (a Sanrio® company).
All rights reserved.
Used Under License.

SIL-5018

GROSSET & DUNLAP
Penguin Young Readers Group
An Imprint of Penguin Random House LLC

Little Miss Naughty™ and © 1981 THOIP (a Sanrio® company). All rights reserved.
First published by Price Stern Sloan, an imprint of Penguin Random House LLC. This edition
published in 2017 by Grosset & Dunlap, an imprint of Penguin Random House LLC,
345 Hudson Street, New York, New York 10014. GROSSET & DUNLAP
is a trademark of Penguin Random House LLC. Printed in the USA.

www.mrmen.com

ISBN 9780843178425

25 24 23 22

Little Miss
Bossy

 Little Miss
Naughty

Little Miss
Neat

 Little Miss
Sunshine

Little Miss
Tiny

 Little Miss
Trouble

 Little Miss
Giggles

 Little Miss
Helpful

 Little Miss
Magic

Little Miss
Shy

Little Miss
Splendid

Little Miss
Twins

 Little Miss
Chatterbox

Little Miss
Ditzy

 Little Miss
Late

 Little Miss
Lucky

 Little Miss
Scatterbrain

Little Miss
Star

 Little Miss
Busy

Little Miss
Quick

Little Miss
Wise

 Little Miss
Tidy

Little Miss
Greedy

Little Miss
Fickle

 Little Miss
Brainy

Little Miss
Stubborn

Little Miss
Curious

Little Miss
Fun

 Little Miss
Contrary

 Little Miss
Somersault

 Little Miss
Scary

 Little Miss
Bad

 Little Miss
Whoops

 Little Miss
Princess

Little Miss
Hug

 Little Miss
Fabulous

$4.99 US
($6.99 CAN)

ISBN 978-0-8431-7842-5

GROSSET&DUNLAP
Visit us at penguin.com/youngreaders
and mrmen.com

 Little Miss
Sparkle

EAN

9 780843 178425

5 0 4 9 9 >